SPONGEBOB SQUAREPANTS

MAN SPONGE SAVES THE DAY

by Sarah Willson
illustrated by The Artifact Group

Ready-to-Read

Simon Spotlight/Nickelodeon
New York   London   Toronto   Sydney

Based on the TV series *SpongeBob SquarePants*® created by Stephen Hillenburg
as seen on Nickelodeon®

SIMON SPOTLIGHT
An imprint of Simon & Schuster Children's Publishing Division
1230 Avenue of the Americas, New York, New York 10020

Manufactured in the United States of America
First Edition
2 4 6 8 10 9 7 5 3 1
Library of Congress Cataloging-in-Publication Data
Willson, Sarah.
Man Sponge saves the day / by Sarah Willson. – 1st ed.
p. cm. – (Ready-to-read. Level 2 ; #15)
"Based on the TV series SpongeBob SquarePants® created by Stephen Hillenburg as seen on Nickelodeon®."
Level 2 Ready-to-Read SpongeBob SquarePants
ISBN-13: 978-1-4169-5936-6   ISBN-10: 1-4169-5936-X
I. SpongeBob SquarePants (Television program) II. Title.
PZ7.W6845Man 2009   [E]-dc22   2007050345

"Aha! They are leaving town!"
said Plankton as he cackled.
"I will invite all the bad guys
to Bikini Bottom!"
He got on the phone and hit
every number on his speed dial.

The bad guys arrived quickly.
"Welcome, fellow do-no-gooders!"
said Plankton. "Mermaidman and
Barnacleboy are out of town.
Now we can take over the world!"
All the bad guys nodded and
laughed.

"And with those two out of the way,
I can finally get my hands on
that Krabby Patty formula!"
Plankton added to himself.

"I think I will go for a bike ride,"
said SpongeBob.
He looked around for
the invisible bicycle.

Three hours later, SpongeBob
found the bicycle.
He opened the garage door
and yelled, "Oh, no!"

Bikini Bottom was in big trouble!
"Help!" everyone cried.
"Where are Mermaidman
and Barnacleboy?"

Everyone was so scared,
they were leaving Bikini Bottom.
Even the police were running away!
SpongeBob knew that it was
up to him to save the day.
"This," he said, "is a job for . . ."

NOW
LEAVING
BIKINI
BOTTOM

"Man Sponge!"

"Off I go to defend the weak, protect the helpless, and fight evil!" said Man Sponge. "To the invisible bicycle!"

"Wait. Where did I park it?" And one hour later, off he went.

"Stop, thief!" shouted Man Sponge.

But the thief did not stop.

"Well, that didn't work,"

Man Sponge said. "What do I do now?"

Just then the thief tripped over
the invisible bicycle.
The bag of money flew into
Man Sponge's hands.
"I did it!" he cried happily.
"Help!" someone else shouted.

Some bad guys had tied up
the ice-cream guy—and Patrick!
The bad guys were pushing all the
ice-cream tubs out of the truck!

Man Sponge crept up to the truck
and took the bad guys' rope.
Twirling it like a lasso, he caught
the two guys and tied them up.
Then he untied Patrick and the
ice-cream man.

Man Sponge saw someone ring
a doorbell, then run away.
He saw Man Ray pop bubble wrap
in the library!
He saw someone else paint on a sign.
"Freeze!" yelled Man Sponge.
But no one froze.

All these bad guys were heading
toward Man Sponge.
So he squirted bubble-blowing liquid
on the ground.

"Whoa!" yelled the bad guys.
They slipped and slid
on the bubble stuff—
right into Man Sponge's
huge jellyfishing net!

Suddenly Man Sponge heard "Help!"
It was Mr. Krabs.
"Somebody has stolen the secret
    Krabby Patty formula!"
he yelled.

"It must be Plankton!" said Man Sponge.
He sprang into action.

"Stop, Plankton!" yelled Man Sponge.
But Plankton did not stop.
Man Sponge pulled something
out of his costume.
TWANG! His tightie-whities
knocked Plankton down.

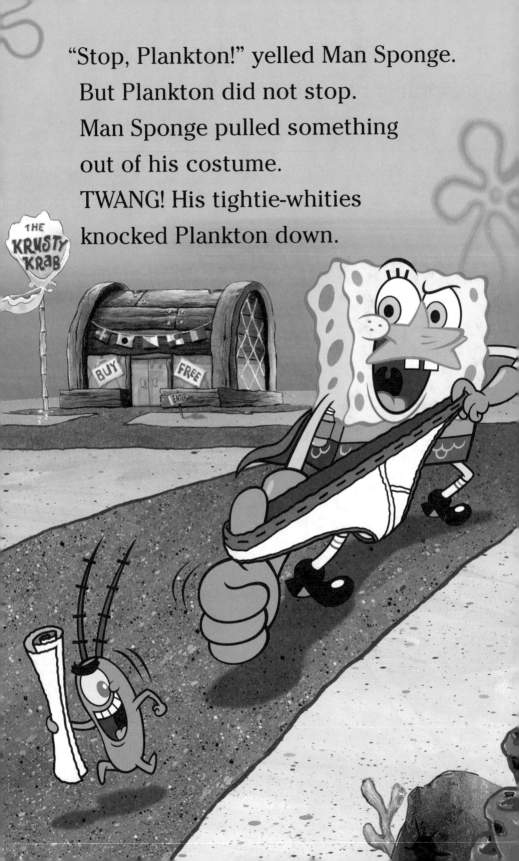

Man Sponge trapped Plankton.
"That should hold you
until the police return," he said.
"I will get you next time, Man Sponge,"
said Plankton.

At last, all was well
in Bikini Bottom.
Everyone came back.
So did the police.
They put the bad guys behind bars.

Two weeks later, Mermaidman and
Barnacleboy returned.
"How was everything?"
asked Mermaidman.
"Oh, just fine," said SpongeBob.
"Everything was under control!"